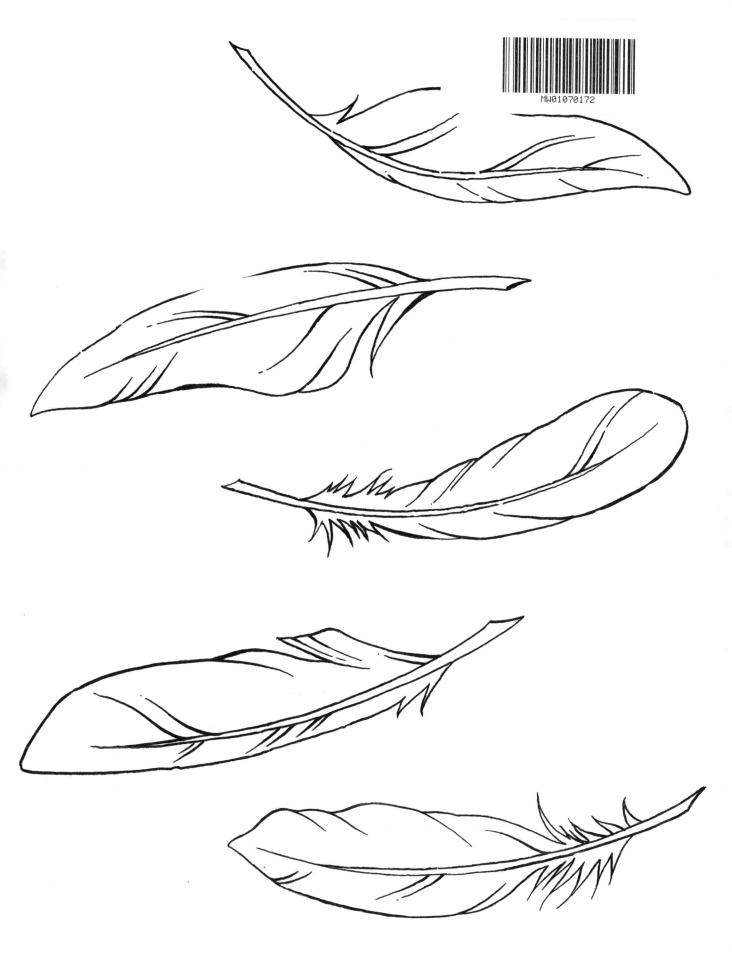

The Gift of Gerbert's Feathers

To Bravery, Marmee, and Opa: may Psalm 91:4 carry and comfort you—*MW*

To my mom, who sculpted her image of Gerbert out of clay the day she first read this story. To Sylvan, for his unwavering support. To Marisa and Brett, whose love sustains me and whose resilience inspires me. And to my greatest teachers, the children and families I have had the honor of working with, who have shown me an abundance of extraordinary beautiful human moments—*LW*

For Angelo: an exceptional person—*MB*

Books for Kids From the
American Psychological Association

© 2020 American Psychological Association. No claim of rights in the U.S. to the underlying content which was authored by one or more U.S. government employees. Illustrations copyright © 2020 by Mikki Butterley. Please contact the publisher for reprints. Except as permitted under the United States Copyright Act of 1976, the cover art, illustrations, and Note to Readers may not be reproduced or distributed in any form or by any means, including, but not limited to, the process of scanning and digitization, or stored in a database or retrieval system, without the prior written permission of the publisher.

Magination Press is a registered trademark of the American Psychological Association. Order books at maginationpress.org or call 1-800-374-2721.

Book design by Gwen Grafft

Printed by Phoenix Color Corporation, Hagerstown, MD

Library of Congress Cataloging-in-Publication Data
Names: Weaver, Meaghann, author. | Wiener, Lori, author. |
    Butterley, Mikki, illustrator.
Title: The gift of Gerbert's feathers / by Meaghann Weaver &
    Lori Wiener ; illustrated by Mikki Butterley.
Description: Washington, DC : Magination Press, [2020] |
    "American Psychological Association." | Summary : Gerbert,
    a special young goose, prepares for his death by whispering
    words of power to his flight feathers and giving them to
    family and friends before his final migration.
Identifiers: LCCN 2018033326| ISBN 9781433830235
    (hardcover) | ISBN 143383023X (hardcover)
Subjects: | CYAC: Terminally ill—Fiction. | Geese—Fiction. |
    Birds—Migration—Fiction.
Classification: LCC PZ7.1.W41775 Gif 2020 | DDC [E]—dc23
LC record available at https://lccn.loc.gov/2018033326

Manufactured in the United States of America
10 9 8 7 6 5 4 3 2 1

The Gift of Gerbert's Feathers

By **Meaghann Weaver, MD, MPH, FAAP &**
Lori Wiener, PhD, DCSW

Illustrated by **Mikki Butterley**

Magination Press • Washington, DC • American Psychological Association

Dear Reader,

This book is written for children like you, children who might have an illness that they worry about. It is also written for children who may be worried about someone they love who is living with a serious illness. It is sometimes hard to tell people about our worries. It can feel easier to keep our worries inside. But keeping worries inside can cause problems too—like loneliness, anger, sadness, and even more fear.

Find a quiet time and a cozy place to cuddle up with someone you are comfortable with to read. You may choose to only read one or two pages a day. You may want to read the book over and over again. You might like the pictures most of all! What is most important is that you know that it is ok to ask questions, to share concerns or fears, and to talk about thoughts that you may not have spoken about with anyone else before. We hope that Gerbert brings you a new way of thinking about illness, death, and family love. Remember, there are people who care about you and will help you along the way.

Meaghann Weaver & Lori Wiener

An extensive Note to Parents & Caregivers, as well as printable feather coloring sheets, is available online at www.apa.org/pubs/magination/441B266

From the moment his eggshell cracked,
and his bill first peeked out,
everyone knew Gerbert was a special goose.

Gerbert tried to fly
from the moment he hatched.
"Adventurous," his mom declared.
"Courageous," his dad agreed.
"Adorable," they both honked.

Gerbert felt safe and warm in his nest.
It was filled with family and love.

Each night the whole flock sang together:
"In sun and rain and ice and snow,
feather to feather, we're always together."

Gerbert was a joyful gosling.
Gerbert and his friends splashed in
shallow water and swam in the
lake. They played chase in open
grasslands, flapping their wings wide
to tickle each other. They waddled
in a line after Gerbert, playing follow
the leader in the grain field.

Gerbert grazed on grass.
Gerbert snacked on sedges.
Gerbert munched on
skunk cabbage leaves.

Gerbert was
especially fond
of blueberries.

He was the best
at removing kernels
from corncobs.

Yet, no matter how much Gerbert ate, he
barely gained weight. As his siblings grew,
Gerbert kept his shorter neck and smaller bill.

But Gerbert felt strong. Gerbert felt vibrant.

Every year, Gerbert's family migrated
south with thousands of other geese.
The huge V-shaped flocks filled the sky.

Gerbert's wings were shorter, so he
had to flap faster than other geese. But he
always kept up in the Great Migration.

As they flew, they
would sing: "In sun and
rain and ice and snow,
feather to feather,
we're always together."

Flying in front takes the most energy, so leading the
V was a special honor reserved for the strongest.

Gerbert's dad was often at the front. He led the flock.

One year, Gerbert's dad called back to Gerbert to join
him. Gerbert had fallen behind, but he gathered
all of his energy to catch up. He flapped and flapped.

As Gerbert reached the front, his dad's strong wings lifted the air around him. Gerbert looked behind him and saw his community—his family, his neighbors, his friends.

He was leading them all.

The next season, Gerbert felt
less hungry, even for blueberries.
He was too tired to play or honk.
His droppings were watery.
His feathers were falling out.

Gerbert had always felt small but strong.
Now he felt fatigued and frail.

He could only watch while his siblings and friends played.
But when he remembered leading the V, he felt proud and strong.

One morning Gerbert overheard his uncle ask
his dad, "Will he migrate this spring?" Gerbert
pretended he couldn't hear their whispered honks.

"His body is weak, but we would never leave him,"
Gerbert's dad said. "We will keep trying to heal and
comfort him, but he may die before the winter flight.
I know we're sad, but we need to be strong for Gerbert."

Gerbert worried his family would miss him,
but was relieved his body would not have
to join the migration. He felt comfort
thinking that he would again
be with his grandmother
who had died years ago.

Gerbert noticed his dad was being more protective.
His mom was making sure to bring him the
freshest blueberries and the largest corn kernels.

His siblings were not drawing the migration
map with him like they used to, and his
friends were not coming to play any more.

Gerbert felt lonely. He
wished someone would ask
him how he was feeling.
He wanted to talk about the
way his beak felt dry and
his neck felt heavy.

The weather started changing, and Gerbert knew that his body would not be able to join his flock in flight. But he wanted his family to know they could always close their eyes and imagine taking flight together. He needed to know he would always be remembered as a strong goose who loved his family and who led the V.

"I know what I can do," thought Gerbert. "I will share
a part of myself. I will share my feathers!" Each day
before the migration, Gerbert lifted a fallen feather
from his nest. Into each feather he whispered a word.

For his dad, he whispered:
"protective strength."
For his mom, he whispered:
"comfort."

For his four siblings,
he whispered:
"joy, growth, peace, and courage."
For his grandfather, he whispered:
"wisdom."
For his neighbor, he whispered:
"gratitude."

For his teacher, he whispered: "patience."
For the bully goose on the river bend, he whispered: "forgiveness."
For his friends, he whispered: "hope and loving-kindness."
For his aunt and uncle, he whispered: "forever and ever."

When the time felt right, Gerbert and his
family shared their thoughts and fears.

Gerbert told his loved ones that he worried they would be too sad to fly without him. He wanted them to take flight together, to be safe and happy, and to always have something to remember him by. Then, one by one, Gerbert shared his feathers.

Gerbert's whole family cuddled close. Each goose put one of their own feathers around him and honked their final goodbye, giving him permission to let go. He felt warm, safe, and peaceful. Together they honked, "In sun and rain and ice and snow, feather to feather, we're always together." Gerbert closed his tired eyes. He felt relief.

Gerbert honked his last "I love you" and gave himself permission to enter into death as his Final Migration, just as winter was arriving.

Gerbert's family and friends each tucked Gerbert's gifted feather into their wings and lifted into the sky. They circled Gerbert's nest and honked, honked, honked. Gerbert's dad took the lead—protective strength leading comfort, joy, growth, peace, and courage. Wisdom, gratitude, patience, forgiveness, hope, loving-kindness, and forever followed.

Every year, the geese return to Gerbert's final resting place, carrying his gifts and honking their song:

"In sun and rain and ice and snow,
feather to feather, we're always together."

About the Authors

Meaghann Weaver, MD, MPH, FAAP, is a pediatric oncologist and chief of the Division of Palliative Care at the Children's Hospital and Medical Center in Omaha, Nebraska. She works with a wonderful interdisciplinary Hand in Hand team which strives to foster the strengths and graces of children and families in the Heartland. Dr. Weaver's favorite life moments are spent painting, dancing, cooking, and gardening with her amazing daughter, Bravery. Dr. Weaver dreams of one day returning to Africa with her family.

Lori Wiener, PhD, DCSW, is co-director of the Behavioral Science Core and head of the Psychosocial Support and Research Program at the pediatric oncology branch of the National Cancer Institute. As both a clinician and behavioral scientist, Dr. Wiener has dedicated her career to applying what she has learned from her work with seriously ill children and their families to create new therapeutic, communication, and educational tools. She lives in Annapolis, Maryland with her family, as well as several animals, including a rescue pup named Tessa, a rescue cat named Tupelo, and a pond filled with goldfish, koi, and noisy frogs. One of Dr. Wiener's favorite pastimes is photographing the migration of snow geese.

About the Illustrator

Mikki Butterley has illustrated everything from greetings cards, to bibles for children, to picture books. She studied graphic design at Blackpool College of Art and Design, after which she worked for a local greeting card company, learning the skills of emboss, die-cut and foil drawings (no computers in those days!), and eventually moved on to freelance illustrating. She then spent 10 years as a senior in-house artist for Hallmark greeting cards before moving back to freelancing to have more time to travel and be with family. Her favorite places to visit are old halls and castles (especially their gardens!), her family's cabin in England's Lake District, and anywhere with a jungle. She lives with her family in South Yorkshire, England.

About Magination Press

Magination Press is the children's book imprint of the American Psychological Association. Through APA's publications, the association shares with the world mental health expertise and psychological knowledge. Magination Press books reach young readers and their parents and caregivers to make navigating life's challenges a little easier. It's the combined power of psychology and literature that makes a Magination Press book special. Visit www.maginationpress.org.